MW01035699

GiRL DAD

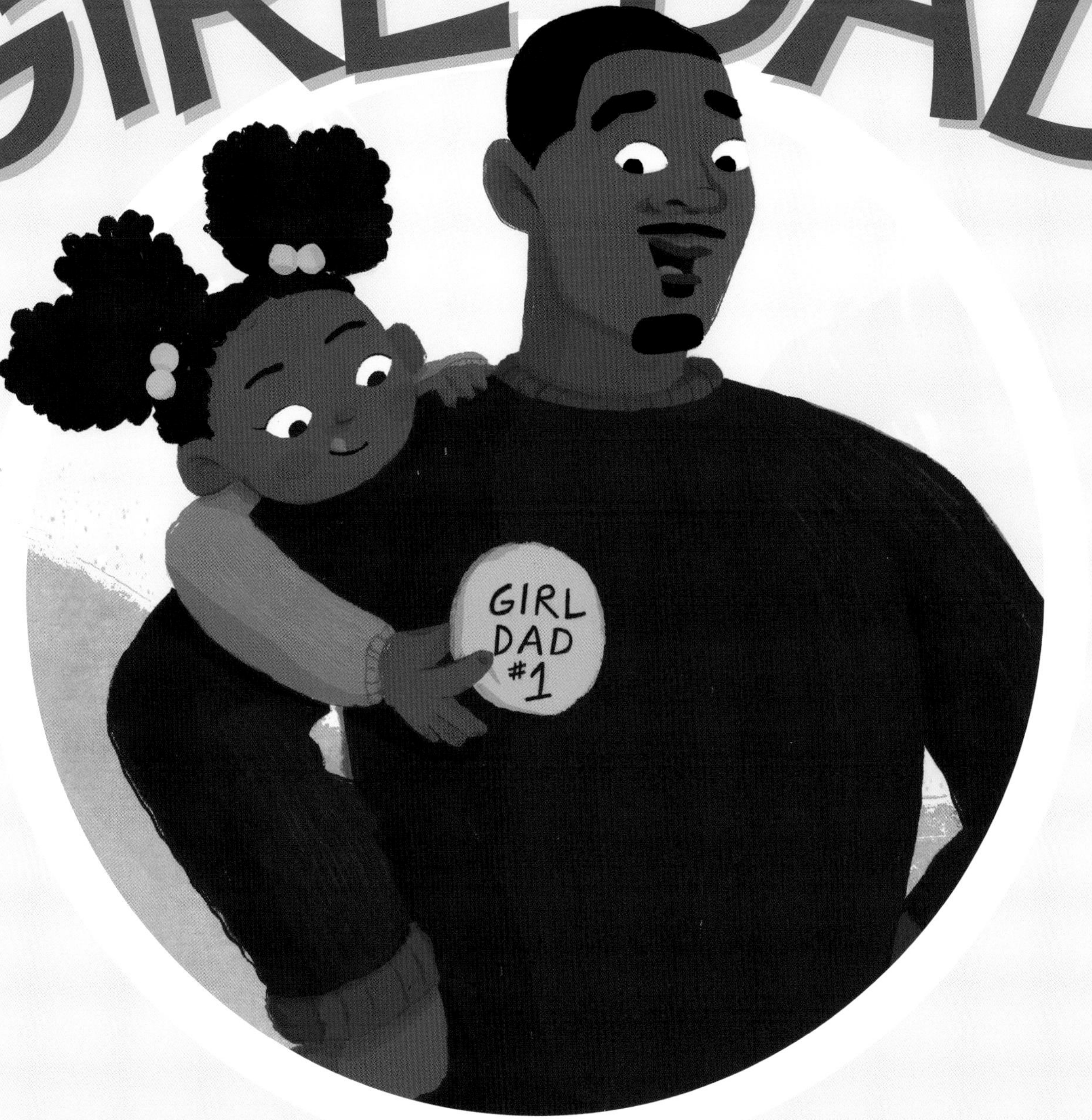

To my daughters, Davynn Williams
and Cameron Williams—S.W.

For Ja'Mari and Ja'leah, my little hearts—J.D.

Girl Dad
Text copyright © 2022 by Sean Williams
Illustrations copyright © 2022 by Jay Davis
Special thanks to Luana Kay Horry
All rights reserved. Printed in the United States of America.
No part of this book may be used or reproduced in any manner whatsoever without written permission
except in the case of brief quotations embodied in critical articles and reviews. For information address
HarperCollins Children's Books, a division of HarperCollins Publishers, 195 Broadway, New York, NY 10007.
www.harpercollinschildrens.com

Library of Congress Control Number: 2021941316
ISBN 978-0-06-311363-3

The artist used pencils and gouache on watercolor paper, and Procreate to create the digital illustrations for this book.
Typography by Chelsea C. Donaldson
22 23 24 25 26   PC   10 9 8 7 6 5 4 3 2 1
❖
First Edition

GIRL DAD

written by Sean Williams ❤ illustrated by Jay Davis

HARPER
An Imprint of HarperCollinsPublishers

There are some things about a girl dad
that I think the world should know.

Like . . .

he looks his best in purple or pink
and can even rock a bow.

He's not afraid to be on point
or to paint your fingernails.

He volunteers to do your makeup,
your braids, and your ponytails!

Girl dad is great for kissing boo-boos and wiping away your tears.

He teaches you to be brave and strong and can help you face your fears.

He shares a love for bright unicorns
and pretty things that glitter.

He scares away the hungry monsters

and catches creepy critters.

He knows how to throw a tea party
and plays dollhouse like a pro.

He will teach you how to kick a ball
and to catch and pitch like so.

A girl dad is serious and tough!

But he has a soft side, too.

He will always catch you when you fall
and stick by your side like glue.

He is your number one biggest fan

GO, BABYGIRL!

and knows how to cheer you on!

He'll learn every single note and word
to the latest princess songs.

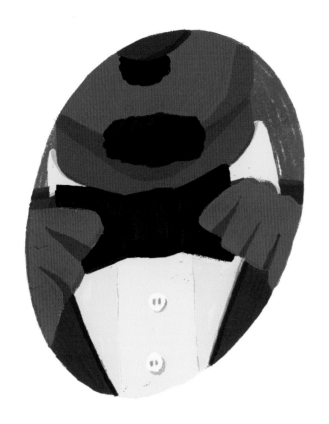

He gets all dressed up

and suited for

BRUSH
BRUSH
BRUSH

the daddy-daughter dance,

where he whispers to you as you start:
"No one even stands a chance!"

He plans the best daddy-daughter dates.
He picks your favorite flower.

He lets you make your own decisions

and show off your girl power.

FLASH

He makes sure you know just what you're worth—
that you keep your standards high.

He will lift you up above his head,
make you feel like you can fly.

He'll remind you that you're beautiful—
that you're also very smart.

Girl dad's the one who has your back
and had it from the start.

HALLOWEEN `21

He was meant to be a girl dad, so you are his motivation.

You give him superdaddy powers and daily inspiration.

There's nothing a girl dad won't do—
he will always be so proud.

You'll know a girl dad when you spot one,
'cause he stands out in a crowd.

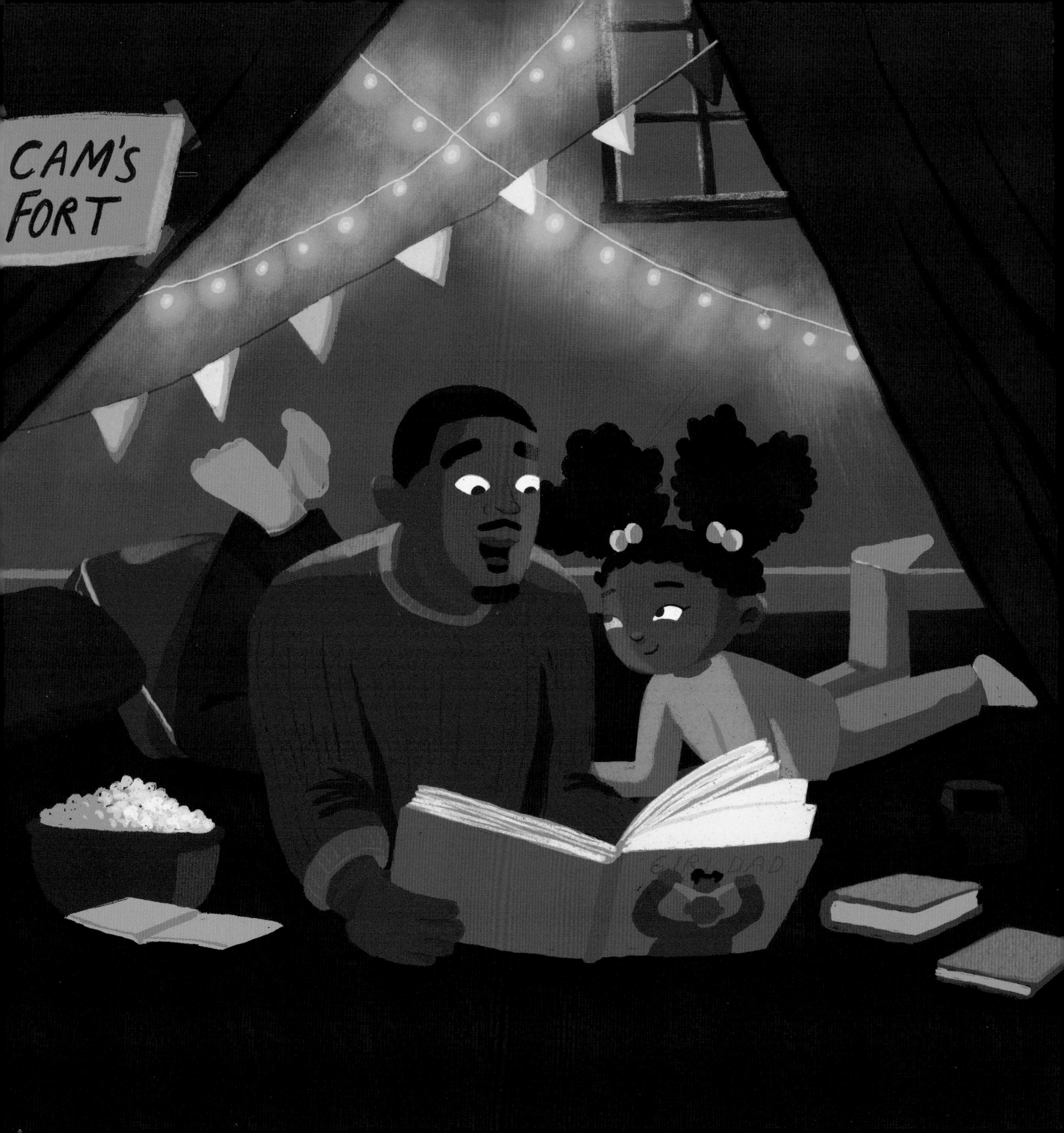
CAM'S
FORT

He loves to cuddle and snuggle up
and hug with all his might.
He kisses you a million times
before he says goodnight.

Above and beyond, that's where he'll go
to give you the whole wide world.
To the moon and back, then back again—
anything for baby girl!

So, if you ever see a girl dad,
just make sure you let him know

how absolutely gorgeous he looks . . .

while rocking that big pink bow.